www.dragonbloodpirates.co.uk

ORCHARD BOOKS
338 Euston Road, London NW1 3BH

First published in 2008 by Lothian Children's Books,
an imprint of Hachette Livre Australia
First published in the UK in 2011 by Orchard Books

ISBN 978 1 40830 823 3

A CIP catalogue record for this book is available from the British Library.

10 9 8 7 6 5 4 3 2 1

Printed in Great Britain by CPI Bookmarque, Croydon

Orchard Books is a division of Hachette Children's Books,
an Hachette UK company.

www.hachette.co.uk

The Deathless Pirate King

Dan Jerris

ORCHARD BOOKS

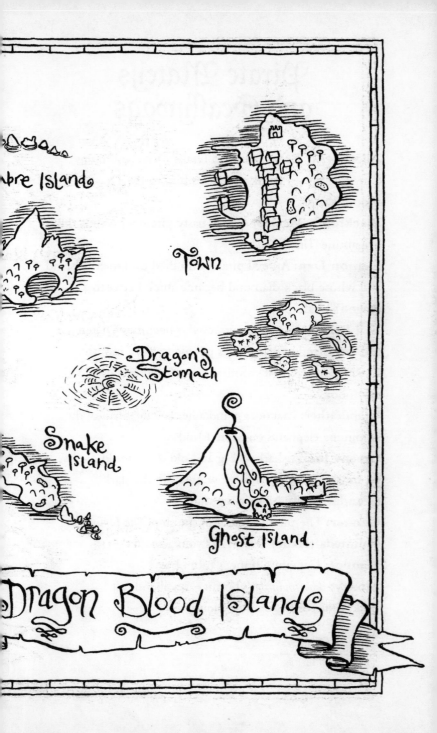

bre Island

Town

Dragon's
Stomach

Snake
Island

Ghost Island.

Dragon Blood Islands

Pirate Mateys and Scallywags

Alleric (Al) Breas: Lives in Drake Drive and owns a mysterious sea trunk that takes him to the Dragon Blood Islands

Blacktooth McGee: A very nasty pirate who runs the brigantine *The Revenge*

Demon Dan: An evil pirate who died on Dragon Island and whose black diamond became stuck between a dragon's teeth

Evil Pearl: A deathless pirate who becomes Queen of Pearl Island and sacrifices people to a sea monster

Flash Johnny: Blacktooth's devious and greedy cabin boy

Grandfather: Mahoot's grandfather and guardian of the swimming elephants on Sabre Island

Greeny Joe: A shark so big and old that mould grows on his skin, making him glow green in the dark

Grenda: Snotty Nell's daughter

Gunner: The pirate captain of the ship *The Invincible*

Halimeda (Hally) Breas: Al's younger sister

Mahoot: Captain Gunner's cabin boy

Mozzy: *The Invincible*'s bosun – small and fast

Jack Seabrook: Al's best friend

Pigface McNurt: Blacktooth's bosun; a huge pirate with a ring through his nose

Prince Alleric: The prince who once ruled Sabre Island but disappeared in mysterious circumstances

Princess Haree: The princess of Ruby Island

Razor Toe: A deathless pirate who has enslaved the people of Ruby Island

Sharkbait: Snotty Nell's one-legged bosun

Slicer: *The Invincible*'s cook

Snakeboot: A magical white three-legged cat with purple eyes. Legend has it he once belonged to a terrifying pirate called Vicious Victor.

Snotty Nell: A horrible one-eyed pirate who sails a worn-out Indiaman called *Nausi VIII*

Stanley Spong: A crooked, sneaky trader in town who cheats people

Vampire Zu: Snotty Nell's huge first mate

Velvetfoot: A fearsome pirate distinctive for his velvet shoes that let him creep up on his victims unannounced

Vicious Victor: A pirate ghost. He used to pillage the Dragon Blood Islands and stole the magical sabre and scabbard that belonged to Prince Alleric.

Grandfather's Tales

Al Breas and Jack Seabrook found themselves in an untidy room stacked to the ceiling with storage chests and smelling of pickled herrings and salted pork. The surge of the ocean, the floor pitching under their feet and the now-familiar creaking of rigging told them they were on board a sailing ship.

Only seconds earlier they had disappeared

from Al's house at number five Drake Drive, in the twenty-first century. They had dressed themselves in their pirate clothes, acquired on one of their recent trips, climbed into Al's grandfather's old sea trunk in the attic and, as they had done many times before, travelled through space and time to the Dragon Blood Islands.

"I was hoping we'd land on Sabre Island," Jack complained.

"Shhh," warned Al. "Keep quiet. We might be on Blacktooth's boat. He'd kill us if he finds us, especially as I'm wearing the Dragon Blood Sabre."

"Sorry," Jack apologised, "you're right. We'll hide here. We should be safe."

"Unless someone comes for supplies," said Al. "It looks like we're in a storeroom."

The words had no sooner left his lips than footsteps clumped outside and the latch lifted. The boys just managed to hide behind a large barrel as the door swung open.

"Mahoot, come here!" bellowed a familiar voice. "I thought you were gunner tidy this room!"

"Captain Gunner!" the boys cried as they leapt from their hiding place and confronted a tall pirate.

The pirate jumped back in shock, drawing his sword instinctively. Then he recognised Al and Jack and lowered his weapon. "You rotten rapscallions!"

he exclaimed. "We've been searching everywhere for you. Why didn't you tell me you were on board?"

"Blacktooth was after us," lied Jack, his face reddening. The pirate didn't know about the magical way Jack and Al transported themselves.

Captain Gunner's voice dropped to a whisper. "Of course. The word is out that you've found the Dragon Blood Sabre. It was a wise idea to sneak on board."

Gunner was interrupted by a barefoot boy who came into the room.

"Mahoot!" Al and Jack cheered, and the boys did a high five.

A three-legged cat bounded in behind the boys, wound itself around Al's and Jack's legs and purred loudly.

"Snakeboot came on board without you," Gunner told them. "That's when we really got worried. If we'd known you'd been stowing away, we'd have had smiles on our faces."

"Where are we sailing to?" asked Al, keen
to change the subject.

"We're off to see Mahoot's grandfather
and take him a few supplies," replied Gunner.

"Wait till Grandfather hears we've found
the Dragon Blood Sabre!" Mahoot said. "And
the Scabbard of Invincibility!"

Later that night, the boys sat in Mahoot's
grandfather's house. Outside, the elephants
trumpeted in the jungle. Al's magical sabre
and scabbard lay on a table and the old man
inspected them in amazement. "I never
thought I would see these treasures again,"
he gasped.

"It's a shame their magical powers have
been lost," said Mahoot. "The sabre can't
make you fly anymore."

"And the scabbard sure isn't a Scabbard of
Invincibility," added Al as he picked it up and

turned it over, showing a small tear in the side and four empty clasps where jewels had once glittered.

"Its four black diamonds are gone," said Mahoot's grandfather. "The scabbard will never work without the diamonds."

"Vicious Victor told us he pulled the diamonds off the scabbard and gave them to four of his crew," explained Jack.

"So we might be able to find the diamonds," Al said hopefully. "And

Vicious Victor said that Snakeboot would
help us restore all of Prince Alleric's treasures.
He even gave us each a ring that he once
stole." He held up his thumb and a ruby-eyed
dragon ring glittered in the firelight.

Jack did likewise, showing off his diamond
and sapphire star-ring, whilst Mahoot
proudly held out his elephant-head ring.

"I did notice your rings," the old man said.
"And I have been wondering about that cat.
It's a most unusual animal."

"Snakeboot's helped us find all sorts of treasures," said Mahoot.

"You never know, the pirates may have buried the diamonds somewhere," Al said. "Snakeboot'll help us find them, I'm sure."

"The diamonds won't be buried," Mahoot's grandfather stated matter-of-factly. "They will still be worn by the very pirates they were given to."

"But they'd be dead by now," said Mahoot. "Vicious Victor was a ghost and the others were well and truly old."

"I's afraid you are wrong. You see the diamonds carry a curse."

"What curse?" asked Jack. His eyes lit up with curiosity.

The aging man drew closer to the boys and whispered, "As a child I was told that the diamonds were made from dragon scales, forged by a magician on a remote island. The magician was an ancestor of Prince Alleric.

The Alleric family were trained to use the
scabbard and sabre wisely. They knew about
the curse." Mahoot's grandfather paused and
looked off into the distance, remembering a
time long before the boys were born.

"So?" the boys chorused.

"So," he replied, shaking his head and focusing on the damaged scabbard in front of him, "the curse dictates that if a bad man should possess one of the scabbard's diamonds, the diamond will possess him in return."

"I don't understand," said Mahoot.

Mahoot's grandfather leaned forward and his voice trembled. "The diamonds are black for a reason – to remind us there is darkness in all our hearts. But in the wrong hands, the diamonds can make the darkness grow. The pirates who were given the diamonds were already bad. Once they touched the black diamonds they would start to think of nothing else but those diamonds. They would wear them at all times, and the more they wore them, the nastier they would become. Their addiction to the diamonds would grow. The magical power of the diamonds, in return, would make the pirates deathless."

"Deathless," breathed Jack. "That sounds cool."

"Why would it sound cool?" asked the old man in surprise. "How does such a curse sound cold?"

"He means it sounds neat," explained Al.

"Neat?" Mahoot and his grandfather stared at each other, totally bewildered.

"We mean it sounds fun," Al finally clarified.

"It is not fun!" Mahoot's grandfather snapped. "It is a curse. Deathless means you never die, but you grow old and ugly, and if you're hurt, the wounds stay there, gaping and bloodless, for ever. You are not invincible. Imagine being gutted, and still alive. How terrible! The diamonds in the wrong hands are cursed. And it is a horrible curse indeed!"

"So what would happen if the diamonds were on the scabbard?" asked Al.

"The four diamonds placed together on the scabbard make their owner invincible, impervious to falls and wounds, but only while they wear the sheath," Mahoot's grandfather explained.

"So why didn't Prince Alleric become bad? Didn't he wear the scabbard all the time?"

"Prince Alleric didn't let the diamonds control him. He knew that people should die in their own time. He understood that death was natural and not to be feared. He kept the scabbard and sabre safe in the castle and not with him. Each generation of princes inherited the pair and they used the magic wisely, for the good of all."

"But is that how Prince Alleric lost it?" probed Al. "By not wearing it?"

"Yes." The old man sighed. "Prince Alleric kept it in his bedroom. He only wore it when he travelled to distant lands. That is why it was easy for Vicious Victor to steal it."

"And the Dragon Blood Sabre?" Al asked. "How does it work?"

"There were magical words," replied Mahoot's grandfather. "But they were only told to the heirs of Sabre Island. When the sabre was stolen, Prince Alleric and Princess Halimeda left Sabre Island and never returned. The magical words went with them."

"We might get lucky and find at least one of the diamonds if we search their castle," said Jack. "It would be fun to be deathless every now and then."

"Fun?" Mahoot's grandfather glared at them. "You boys have an odd idea of fun." His voice dropped in warning. "Remember, it would not be fun to meet whoever has the diamonds."

"How about dinner?" suggested Mahoot, breaking up the conversation. "I don't know about you, but I'm starving."

"I apologise," said the old man. "I've been frightening you with terrible tales of curses. Now is a time to celebrate. The sabre is found and it is wonderful to have you boys back. We should eat. Tomorrow I must give Captain Gunner something special I found."

The Message in a Bottle

The next day Mahoot's grandfather presented Captain Gunner with a barnacle-encrusted bottle that had a rolled parchment inside.

Gunner opened the bottle, unrolled the parchment and studied it. "It's a map," he told the eagerly awaiting boys, "with this note written on it:

"'Help us. We are captives on Ruby Island.

We will be sold as slaves. Once we owned great treasure. If you free us the treasure will be yours.' It's signed, 'Princess Haree of Ruby Island.'"

"I've heard of Ruby Island before," said Gunner. "The villagers mined rubies and hid them on another island in a maze of reefs and tidal rips, and their king had a huge ruby in his crown."

"I wonder who's taken the princess captive?" Al asked.

"When I was in town I heard a rumour that Stanley Spong was expecting a shipload of slaves," said Gunner, "and I saw him talking to Blacktooth." His eyes narrowed in anger. "It could have been him, the scurvy rascal."

"Should we go and help the princess?" asked Jack.

Gunner's thoughts turned to treasure. "I'd love to get my own back on Blacktooth," he said. Then he shrugged his shoulders. "And who can pass up treasure?"

And so it was that Gunner's ship, *The Dandylion*, lowered anchor in a tiny bay at the north end of Ruby Island. The boys volunteered to go ashore, explore and find out if the information in the princess's note was true.

A short while later, Al, Jack and Mahoot

found themselves in Roseberry, the island's town, which was overlooked by a fortified castle. As they wandered through the winding streets, they noticed Blacktooth's boat, *The Revenge*, swinging at anchor in the bay, but were quickly distracted by the bustle of the markets.

Attracting attention as newcomers to the town, a beggar lifted a bony hand, grabbed at Jack's coat as he passed, and stopped him. "Master," he wailed, "give me alms."

As Jack tried to pull away from the beggar's clutch, the man grasped his hand tightly and his eyes widened in shock. "You're wearing the king's ring!" he cried loudly. "The boy wears the king's ring!"

Held fast by the beggar, Jack looked for a way to escape as a jostling mob soon surrounded him.

Suddenly a man wrenched Jack from the beggar's grip, hoisted him over his shoulder and ran. Al and Mahoot gave chase and soon caught up with the kidnapper. Al threw himself upon the man and shouted, "Let him go!"

"Your friend's wearing the royal ring!" the man bawled defensively. "If Razor Toe hears about it, he'll kill him and take the ring!"

"What are you talking about?" Al demanded.

"I'm protecting your friend," explained the man as he released Jack. "This ring was taken from our island more than seventy years ago, when our king was killed by pirates."

"But I got it from a pirate," said Jack, confused.

"Do you know of a Princess Haree?" Al cut in. "We hear she's been imprisoned and going to be sold as a slave."

The man looked very surprised at Al's words. "Your information is correct. Haree is our princess. She will be sold tomorrow and

28

shipped away. She is held in the dungeons by Razor Toe, the pirate king."

"Razor Toe's a funny name," said Mahoot.

"Razor Toe," the man shuddered at the name, "wears razors in his shoes and can kill people with just a kick. And he has an armed crew of evil cut-throats who serve him."

"Is Blacktooth going to take the slaves away?" asked Jack.

The man nodded sadly.

"We were hoping to free them," Mahoot explained, "but from what you say we don't have time."

"But we could buy time," said Al, thinking aloud. "Mahoot, can you go back to the ship and persuade Gunner to attack Blacktooth's boat? If the boat's damaged he can't take the slaves away."

"What will you and Jack do?" asked Mahoot.

"We'll try to find a way to free the slaves." Al turned to the man who had helped them. "Can you show us the way to the dungeons?"

Escape

The man left Al and Jack hidden in the shadows of an alleyway opposite two pirates who guarded a dungeon door. The smell of baking bread wafted through the air, making the boys hungry.

"Any idea how to free them?" asked Jack, after they had watched the dungeon entrance for a few minutes.

Al shrugged. "None at all."

A loud clatter behind them made them turn. A door opened and a woman brought out a huge tray of burned bread rolls and dumped them in the street.

"I have an idea now!" said Al excitedly. "Quick, pick up the bread and follow me."

Al and Jack carried the burned bread nervously towards the guards. "Food for the slaves," Al announced. "It's from Razor Toe."

The guards didn't even look twice or ask any questions, but moved back and let the boys pass. Al and Jack walked cautiously through the prison until they found the slaves, chained against a long wall, out of sight of their captors.

They handed out the bread until they came to a young woman with proud, flashing eyes. Jack held his hand out towards her so she could see the ring on his thumb. The girl's eyes went wide with surprise.

"Princess Haree?" asked Jack.

The girl nodded.

"We got your message in the bottle," Al whispered. "We've come to save you."

The girl nodded again in understanding and pointed to a nearby room. "The guards keep the keys over there," she murmured.

Al raced to the room, pulled a key from a peg and was back in seconds, undoing the girl's shackles. In turn she freed the slave next to her and handed her the key. "Unshackle everyone," she commanded.

Freed, the prisoners stood nervously before their princess, waiting for instructions.

Jack pulled the ring from his finger and handed it to Haree. "Princess," he said, "I believe this ring is yours."

"It is indeed," she said proudly. "It was once my grandfather's." Her eyes shone with joy as she placed the ring on her thumb. "With this ring I have a chance to help my people," she announced. She turned to those waiting

quietly in front of her. "Follow me," she ordered.

Instead of going towards the dungeon door, however, the princess turned and led them to some stairs that wound into the bowels of the earth.

"We'll be trapped," moaned one of the slaves. "Where is the princess leading us?"

Haree turned, her eyes blazing. She raised

the ring Jack had given her. "I have the king's ring," she said. "Trust me."

Within seconds they came to a solid brick wall, signalling a dead end. Haree's followers began to jostle each other in panic, but the princess ignored them. She reached up and pressed the ring against a carving high on the wall. A gasp rippled through the crowd as a secret door creaked open, revealing a tunnel. "Everyone inside, quickly!" Haree commanded.

The prisoners hurried along the tunnel until they emerged from a doorway into a narrow road.

"Now, run to your families and hide," instructed Haree. The escapees needed no further prompting. They took to their heels, leaving the princess and the boys alone.

"That was clever," said Al in admiration. "How did you know about that tunnel and the secret door? And how did you know the ring would work? It's been missing for more than seventy years!"

"Although he was no longer King of Ruby Island when I was a child, my father taught me all the secrets of the ring and of the castle," said Haree. "At the time, I thought he was stupid, wasting my time telling me of the stolen ring and how to find secret tunnels that I could never use. But as

Razor Toe continued to bully and enslave our people, I dreamt of freeing them. When I grew older I made it my business to learn everything I could about the old secrets. Now..." Her eyes filled with tears. "Now you boys have brought me the ring of my ancestors and given me some power. Finally, all I've learnt has meaning, and I'm glad I listened to my father."

"Where is your father now?" asked Jack.

Haree's lip trembled. "Last year, Razor Toe kidnapped him. I haven't seen him since."

"I'm so sorry, Princess Haree. Maybe we should take you somewhere safe?" Al suggested. "Please come back to our ship with us."

"No," said Haree. "I need to find my father. Will you help me?"

The boys had no time to answer because a group of heavily armed pirates was running down the road towards them.

"They've realised the prisoners have escaped!" said Jack.

"Quick, follow me," said Haree and, to the boys' surprise, she turned back into the tunnel they had just come from.

Razor Toe

Haree led the boys through thickly walled
tunnels that seemed to wind upwards for
ever. Finally the princess stopped and said,
"Before I look for my father, I would like
to give you boys some treasure as a reward,
but I will need your help to reach it."

"That's really kind of you, but where is it?"
asked Jack.

"Behind an evil idol on Vault Island,"
Haree replied.

"An evil idol?" asked Al.

"Razor Toe put an evil idol in front of the vault door to guard the treasure he stole from us," Haree explained. "It's supposed to kill anyone who looks at it, but I don't believe that, because Razor Toe goes to Vault Island all the time, and he's not dead. He put my ruby crown on the idol and I really want to get that back, too."

"We should return to the ship," said Al. "Captain Gunner will take us to Vault Island."

"But it's surrounded by dangerous reefs and currents which have sunk many ships," said Haree, dismissing Al's suggestion. "Besides, I don't want to wait, because Razor Toe already knows I'm free. We need to get there as quickly as we can."

"Do you know another way to Vault Island?" said Al.

Haree nodded. "There's a tunnel that leads from my throne room," she said. "If you come with me we'll be there in minutes.

I could also get my crown from the idol. And once I get my crown from the idol the townspeople will respect me. I'll be able to fight Razor Toe with them by my side."

"I'm not sure that's a good idea," said Al. "I know you need help, but Captain Gunner is coming to fight Blacktooth. We should wait for him."

But Haree didn't want to listen to reason. She stamped her foot, made a huffing sound, turned and ran up the tunnel. "I'm going with or without you," she called over her shoulder.

Jack turned to Al. "Do you know how to get out of here?" he asked.

"No," said Al, "it's a maze. I think we'd best stick with Haree. Maybe we can talk her out of her plans."

The boys raced after the princess. Eventually she stopped beside a small peephole that let light into the tunnel.

She signalled to the boys to look through it.

To Al's surprise a sumptuous room, hung with shiny silk curtains, came into view. A golden throne glittered with flashing rubies, and sitting on the throne was a hideously scarred, skull-faced man. The fingers of one of his hands were missing and a gaping flesh wound seeped on his neck. A black diamond glittered fiercely in his turban and his eyes, dark with evil fire, glared angrily

at Blacktooth, who stood in front of him.

Al nudged Jack. "Look at the diamond," he whispered. "Could that be one of the dragon diamonds from the scabbard?"

"Shhh!" Haree warned. "Our voices might carry."

Blacktooth glowered with fury at Razor Toe. "I've paid for thirty sslaves," he growled, "and I'll ssail tomorrow with them, or you musst return my money with interesst."

Razor Toe leapt to his feet in answer. He kicked out at Blacktooth, his boots whistling through the air. Blacktooth's sword, belt and coat buttons clattered to the floor, and he jumped back in fear.

"Don't tell me what to do!" Razor Toe roared.

"I'm ssorry," Blacktooth grumbled, "but I could have ssold the princesss for a fortune and it'ss not my fault the sslaves have esscaped."

"We'll find her," Razor Toe promised. "I'll put out a big reward. She and her friends won't get the better of me!"

Several minutes later, Blacktooth and Razor Toe left the room through the huge golden double doors.

Haree wasted no time. She pressed her ring into a carving on the tunnel wall and a concealed door sprang open. "Are you coming?" she asked, as she pulled a silken curtain aside and strode into the empty throne room.

"I guess we can't argue with her," said Al, following her.

Jack's eyes widened as they walked past the massive gold and ruby throne.

"That throne should be mine," Haree said haughtily, and to the boys' horror, she climbed up and sat on it.

"My grandfather was killed in this room," she said defiantly, "and I plan to take my throne back."

"You'll be killed here, too, if Razor Toe returns," Al warned.

Suddenly, the golden doors swung open and a guard stood there, open-mouthed at seeing Haree on the throne.

"Intruders in the castle!" he shouted. "Help! Intruders!"

Haree leapt from the throne and dodged behind it. The boys followed as she pulled open another curtain, revealing a diamond-studded door. She flung the door wide and raced down a tunnel lit with torches, Al and Jack following close behind.

Shouts echoed down the passage behind them as they ran.

"We're in trouble now," Jack puffed. "They're after us!"

Trapped

Blacktooth, Razor Toe and a crew of heavily armed pirates thundered in pursuit of Haree and the boys. Haree, older and taller than her companions, lead the way. The pirates' angry shouts gave Al added strength. "Give it all you've got!" he cried, as he overtook Jack.

They came to a three-way junction where the torches no longer flickered. In the diffused grey light, Haree stopped, suddenly confused.

"Which way?" Al asked.

Panicked, Haree made an instant decision
and ran into a darker tunnel. Within minutes
the light vanished and they were forced to
slow down. "I think we took the wrong
path," said Jack.

They stumbled onwards, their hearts
beating in fear, until Al blundered into a
wall. They felt around in the dark, quickly
discovering they had reached a dead end.

The clattering steps of the pirates were coming ever closer.

"We can't go back," Jack said in dismay. "What shall we do?"

"Try to find a carving shaped like a star," Haree ordered. "Hurry!"

The boys began patting the walls high and low, until Al's knuckles brushed against a carving. "Here, I think I've found it!" he called.

Haree used her ring and, to the boys' relief, a small trapdoor creaked outwards, letting in some light.

They scrambled through on their hands and knees. Al turned and tried to pull the door shut behind them, but it was jammed.

"Leave it," said Haree, as the voices of the pirates sounded closer and closer.

Jack took the lead, crawling as fast as he could until he rammed into something crusty and hard. A rotting skull fell to the ground and he found himself tangled in a human skeleton. "Help!" he shrieked.

Haree grabbed the mouldering bones and shoved them away. While she pulled Jack free, they could hear the pirates behind them puffing and groaning as they squeezed themselves through the tiny tunnel. "Don't worry about dead men!" Haree commanded, and she pushed Jack ahead of her.

The tunnel grew bigger and daylight

began to appear. The trio ran recklessly towards the light. But at the entrance they came to an abrupt halt.

A sheer drop lay before them. They were on the edge of a steep cliff, trapped more than ten metres above the ocean. Below them they could see Captain Gunner's ship, *The Dandylion*, tacking against a rapid current and a head wind. Shouts rang out behind them as the pirates collided with the skeleton. Al looked around desperately but there was no escape.

"Can you swim?" he asked Haree.

The princess nodded. Without warning, he grabbed her hand and yelled out to Jack, "Jump!"

Sea Chase

Captain Gunner was on the bridge of
The Dandylion, not far from the town
of Roseberry. His blood was fired with
excitement and he rubbed his hands with
glee as he thought about how he would
soon pull the wind out of Blacktooth's sails.
Something moving at the top of the cliff
nearby caught his eye and he turned his
telescope. To his astonishment he saw Al, Jack
and a girl he'd never seen before leaping from
the precipice. They hit the water with force,

sending a plume of spray into the air.

"Man the lifeboat!" bellowed Gunner. "Come about!"

When Al hit the water the breath was knocked from his body, and he struggled to the surface, gasping for air. Jack was already floating on his back, breathing heavily beside him. Seconds later, Haree surfaced. Her face was pale and her eyes bugged in terror as she fought for breath. Then Al looked up at the cliff and saw Razor Toe and Blacktooth glaring down at them. Razor Toe pointed out to sea, and Al turned his head. *The Dandylion* was changing course and a lifeboat was rowing towards them. They were saved!

Slicer, the cook, and Mozzy, the bosun, soon hauled the trio out of water. Within minutes they were back on board the ship.

"So," Gunner said, once the boys and the princess had caught their breath. "Let me see if I've got this right: you boys freed the slaves and escaped from Razor Toe and now everyone on *The Dandylion*'s gunner fill their pockets with rubies." He smiled at the thought. "Well, that sounds good to me."

"Blacktooth will be after us," warned Al, "and Razor Toe."

"No old five-fingered pirate's gunner get the better of me," said Gunner.

"But Haree said the idol guarding the treasure can kill you," added Jack.

"I told you, it's a silly legend," said Haree.

"I'm not gunner let Blacktooth beat me!" Gunner glanced up at the filling sails. "We've a fair wind, and you, young lady, will show us the way through the reefs."

"I've not been there myself," Haree explained, "but I *have* studied the maps..."

Vault Island became visible from behind a reef surging with foam, just off *The Dandylion*'s bow. The tide pulled the boat sideways, threatening to drag it onto the rocks.

"There's the channel, there," Haree directed.

Gunner steadied the helm, steering towards a ribbon of blue water between the jagged teeth of the reef. The swirling currents twisted their passage and, as sharp rocks scraped against the hull, Gunner heaved on the tiller. "Trim the sails!" he screamed, as the boat slipped back into the open sea. "We're coming about."

A shrill whistle from Mozzy warned them that another boat was approaching.

"Blacktooth," snarled Gunner, glancing over his shoulder and sighting sail. "Curse his scaly hide."

Once again Gunner attempted the channel. This time, with the wind behind and the vicious waves against them, *The Dandylion*'s bowsprit hit the boiling strait, sending spume over the decks. The grinding of a thousand knives on the hull told the crew the ship was in danger.

Gunner let the current take *The Dandylion* back to open water again. Blacktooth's boat was almost upon them, his crew clearly armed with pikes and muskets. A cannon shot whistled over their heads. Blacktooth meant business.

"Third time lucky," Gunner said, gritting his teeth and swinging savagely on the tiller while the sails flapped loudly.

This time they pushed through without incident, but the fierce current on the other side of the reef and the breeze behind them forced Gunner to jibe with full sails.

The Dandylion veered dangerously and Gunner was flung from the wheel. The sails thundered, water poured over the decks and spars snapped. The ship wallowed, helpless.

Just as Gunner managed to regain control, Blacktooth forged through the channel. He fired his cannon and splinters of wood showered across the poopdeck.

Al and Jack ducked for cover.

The Revenge came alongside *The Dandylion* within seconds. "Give up, you sstinking sswine!" shouted Blacktooth.

"To arms!" cried Gunner. His crew grabbed their muskets and fired on *The Revenge*. Smoke swirled through the air and Gunner ordered the topmen into the rigging so they could shoot at Blacktooth from above. Soon the two boats were locked together, firearms booming in fierce combat.

Mid-battle, Haree suddenly pulled on Gunner's coat. "Watch out, there's a big rock just under the water ahead," she warned.

Gunner noted the dark shadow beneath the waves.

"We have to go to the right, the other side is shallow," said Haree.

Gunner gave her a huge grin in thanks, but kept a steady course.

Blacktooth, absorbed in the battle, continued to hold his position alongside.

Gunner waited till the last moment, then signalled the topmen and hauled on the tiller. The topmen flew to the ropes and *The Dandylion* shifted to starboard.

Startled by the manoeuvre, Blacktooth ceased fire. Almost too late, he saw the danger and managed to tack, but was forced to port. Within seconds *The Revenge* came to a grinding halt in the hidden rock and its foresail blew apart with the force of the wind.

Realising they were free of Blacktooth for the moment, the crew of *The Dandylion* cheered and sailed into Vault Island where they dropped anchor. Then, leaving Mahoot, Snakeboot and a small crew to guard the ship, Gunner took Al, Jack, Haree and fifteen heavily armed men ashore.

Fight for Treasure

Al and Jack found themselves climbing through rocky terrain towards the centre of Vault Island, following Haree and trailed by the others. They came to a steep track and, as they climbed, a fierce battle cry stopped them in their tracks.

Several men brandishing swords ran towards them. Razor Toe, wielding a scimitar, leapt down from a boulder, almost knocking Al off his feet.

"Give no quarter!" the dreadful pirate roared.

Gunner jumped in front of Al, his sword arcing in a flash of silver. Razor Toe fought back with his curved weapon, simultaneously lashing out with his foot, leaving a long gash in his opponent's thigh. Gunner fell and Razor Toe moved in for the kill.

With a chill of terror, Al moved quickly, grabbing his sabre and brandishing it before Razor Toe. The ruby in his weapon glinted in the sunlight.

The ghastly pirate king stepped back, his malicious eyes sparkling. The black diamond in his turban glittered. "The Dragon Blood Sabre!" he hissed. "How did you come by Vicious Victor's sabre?"

His question went unanswered, for Mozzy, seeing Gunner lying injured, flung himself at Razor Toe wielding a cutlass. Using all his force, he lashed out, shattering the scimitar and throwing Razor Toe backwards. Realising this was their chance, Gunner staggered to his feet and together he and Mozzy forced their way along the path.

One of Razor Toe's men fell, never to move again, and in the raging battle Haree, who had dodged and weaved between the attackers, managed to grab the fallen man's sword.

She turned, only to find a bloodthirsty pirate looming over her with a knife. She thrust out with the sword, cutting him, but he retaliated and she stumbled. The pirate, livid with rage at being attacked by a girl, hurled his knife at her.

Quicker than lightning Haree ducked and the knife seared past her face, scratching her cheek. She screamed out in pain and the pirate stepped forward, his sword poised to hurt the princess further. But suddenly Slicer appeared from behind and dealt the pirate a final blow. Haree was saved.

Weary, bleeding and desperately fighting to gain ground, Gunner's crew continued upwards towards a stone porch carved into the hillside.

As they neared the large door, Razor Toe stopped. He waved his men back and his eyes glinted mockingly. "The princess leads you to your death," he taunted. "Give her up, and I'll let you live."

"I will not give up," Haree answered. "You are the one who should give up. Wait till I have my crown!"

Razor Toe roared with chilling laughter. "Go on then, princess. You'll never gain the crown, and if you take your friends with you, I will get the Dragon Blood Sabre. But if you give up, I'll let you live."

The princess turned to Gunner. "I will not conceed to this evil pirate. I'm sorry."

Gunner looked into the eyes of the brave girl before him. "Don't be sorry. I came for treasure," he replied, "and treasure I'm gunner have."

Idol of Death

Haree opened the door at the back of the porch and they moved through the entrance towards what they hoped would be the treasure room. Strangely, Razor Toe did not race after them and attack, he onlystayed where he was.

Gunner looked disconcerted. "You know," he said, "once we get the treasure, we're gunner have to fight that maniac all over again to get back to the boat."

"No, we won't," Haree told him. She held

Jack's glittering ring before his eyes. "See this ring? It's the key to a hidden door inside the treasure chamber. But it's not the door that leads back to the castle. That will be heavily guarded and if we try to escape through it we'll be captured. This ring opens a door that Razor Toe knows nothing about. It leads to a secret passage into a cave, further around the island. You can take the reward I give you, enter this tunnel, and return to your boat, and Razor Toe will have no idea!"

This was enough for Gunner. He limped onwards along a brightly painted hallway until another door barred their way. It was painted with a skull and crossbones and the words 'Death to All Who Enter'.

"Razor Toe's certain the evil idol that's guarding the vault will kill us," warned Jack. "*That's* why he's not following us."

"Don't be so sure, " Haree said calmly. "He's not following because he thinks we'll leave from the tunnel on the other side of the vault and try to get to the castle. He'll have guards there waiting to kill us."

Suddenly, one of Gunner's pirates, impatient and eager to reach the treasure, pushed at the door before them. Several other crewmen made to follow.

"Stop!" Al cried. "I think there really is something in there that has the power to kill!"

"Listen to him," Gunner warned. "He's saved our hides before."

"But we can't just stand here jawing all day," argued the pirate. "I want some treasure now and we need to get back to *The Dandylion* fast." He opened the door a crack.

"I'm ordering you to stop!" Gunner roared.

The pirate glared mutinously at Gunner and, ignoring him, continued to open the door.

"Stop at once, you scurvy dog!" Gunner shouted. But his words fell on deaf ears as the pirate marched inside and the door slammed behind him.

"I told you – Razor Toe is only scaring us," Haree said. "He came through that room from the castle. How else did he get onto this island without a ship? There's nothing in there but—"

71

Her words were cut short by a nerve-jangling scream. The door before them was flung open and the pirate reappeared, his eyes bulging in terror. He gagged and grabbed at his throat. "The idol!" he shrieked, slumping to the floor. His body stiffened, the flesh fell from his bones and in seconds a skeleton lay at their feet.

Horrified, everyone turned and began running along the hallway, back towards Razor Toe.

"Stop!" shouted Al, realising that Haree was right and there had to be a way past the idol. "This is just what Razor Toe wants. He'll easily kill us when we come out. He knows we're scared and wounded!"

"I'm not scared!" Gunner bellowed, stopping. The others followed suit.

Al turned to Haree. "You say Razor Toe and his men have been through this room. What does the legend actually say?"

"That the idol kills all who look upon it," she replied.

Al thought about her words for several seconds. "*Look* at it?"

Haree nodded.

"I think I know how Razor Toe gets past," he said.

Hoping with all his might that he was right, Al closed his eyes and, steeling himself, bravely opened the door. Dropping to his knees, he lowered his head, opened his eyes once again and focused on the ground. He crawled slowly forward until he bumped into something solid in his path. Realising this was probably the pedestal of the idol, he continued past until he found another door.

Al stood up gingerly, opened the door and stepped into the treasure room. Before him glittered mounds of gold, piles of pearls and chests brimming with rubies.

Awestruck, Al waited for his heart to return

to its normal beat, then turned, fell to his knees
again and made his way back to the others.

His arrival was greeted with beaming
smiles and clapping.

"We *can* get past. We just need to get on
our hands and knees and crawl," Al said.
"Don't look up, just follow the feet of the
man in front."

Like caterpillars, the pirates were soon
shuffling past the deathly idol and into the
treasure vault.

"Now you can stand up and look around,"
Al said, once they were safe. The pirates
gasped at the sight before their eyes. While
they filled their pockets with jewels, Al helped
Jack bind Gunner's injured leg with some silk

he found in the treasure room. He also found some velvet that had wrapped pearls and pressed it against the gash on Haree's face. She turned her grateful eyes on him. It was then that he remembered her wish.

While everyone was busy, Al quietly left the treasure room. He summoned every last drop of courage, dropped to his knees and crawled to the evil idol. When he reached its base, he shut his eyes and ran his hands up the idol, feeling the cold stone under his fingers, until he came to its head. When he touched metal he knew he had found Haree's crown. Carefully, and with his eyes still shut tight, removed the crown and placed it on his head. Then he leaned against the idol and pushed with all his might until the stone shifted. Determined, he heaved against it again, feeling the idol topple. It crashed to the floor, splintering loudly.

Al turned and scrambled back into the treasure room, slamming the vault door behind him. Proudly he held out the golden crown with its flashing ruby to the surprised princess, and her eyes filled with tears.

The Dragon Diamond

Razor Toe waited half an hour and, when there was no sign of life, smiled to himself. "Wait here," he told his men. "I'll go and collect their remains." He strode assuredly down the passage, a thrill in his heart as he imagined gathering the famed Dragon Blood Sabre from the skeleton that would be lying in front of his deadly idol. Knowing that the evil statue couldn't kill him, he entered the

room. His confidence instantly evaporated.
Before him, the idol lay shattered – and there
was not a skeleton to be seen.

He ran into the vault, finding it empty and
most of the treasure gone. Incredulous, he
hurriedly unlocked the door that led to the
castle and flung it open, disturbing a crew of
sleepy guards. "Where are they?" he screamed.

"No one came through here," one of
them replied.

Razor Toe slammed the heavy door shut
again, turned and ran back to his waiting men.
Just as he burst into the sunshine, gunfire
erupted from the beach.

Minutes earlier and limping heavily, Gunner
had led the way from the cave, his men
grinning from ear to ear at their success.

As soon as they reached the beach, Al
stopped. Not far from the shore were
The Dandylion and, to everyone's surprise,

The Revenge. Blacktooth was standing at the prow of a longboat which moved rapidly towards them. As soon as he sighted Gunner, he aimed his pistol and fired. His crew copied their captain's example and took aim. A volley of shots rocketed through the air.

Everyone who'd escaped the treasure vault raced towards *The Dandylion* for safety. As Al climbed into its longboat, Razor Toe and his henchmen hurled themselves from the clifftop with vicious cries, and Blacktooth collected the pirate king and his men in his vessel.

As Al and Jack gained a foothold on *The Dandylion*'s decks, Gunner realised they wouldn't have time to weigh anchor or set sail before they were boarded by the enemy. "Prepare your weapons," he ordered. "We're gunner have to fight again." His crew waited, muskets primed.

Razor Toe was the first to climb over *The Dandylion*'s rails. He immediately took a bullet to the chest. Yet instead of falling back into the sea, dead as a doornail the dreadful pirate kept walking.

Gunner's crew lurched back in fear. What's more, their terror gave Blacktooth and the other pirates time to clamber on board.

As Razor Toe moved towards him with murder in his eyes, Gunner fired at point-blank range. A dreadful hole opened in the pirate's shirt, but again Razor Toe was oblivious to the wound.

Al realised they were facing a man who wore a dragon's diamond. Razor Toe was a deathless pirate, just as Mahoot's grandfather had warned them.

As Razor Toe closed in on Captain Gunner, it became obvious there was no way to stop his advance. Gunner hobbled backwards and Razor Toe kicked at him.

The blades in his shoes sliced through the air, cutting Gunner once again. The man fell and Razor Toe balanced himself for a deathblow.

Watching in horror, Al pushed over a barrel that stood beside him and rolled it in front of Gunner just as Razor Toe kicked out. The pirate's foot smashed into the barrel, splintering it with the force of his kick.

Thwarted, Razor Toe's attention shot to

Al. His eyes lit up with fire at the sight of the sabre hanging at Al's waist. He lunged forward and grabbed the boy with one hand, his other reaching for the sabre.

Seeing his friend caught fast, Jack threw himself on the deathless pirate, punching at him. But Razor Toe shrugged him off effortlessly, throwing him to the deck.

But as Razor Toe reached to pull the Dragon Blood Sabre from its scabbard, Snakeboot the cat, who had been sunning himself on the cabin roof when all the action had started, leapt upon his head, knocking the turban with the black diamond to the ground.

Razor Toe instantly dropped the sabre, released Al from his death grip and made a frantic grab for his turban. But Jack was too fast. He seized the turban and ran. Razor Toe, still towering over Al, wobbled, stumbled and clutched at his chest as blood poured

from the recent bullet wounds. Then, with a terrible scream, he fell to the deck.

The terrifying cry froze the blood of all who were fighting. Before their eyes the evil pirate king began to sizzle. His eyes bulged out, his lips curled and smoked. Finally the flesh fell from his bones and a stench worse than rotting garbage filled the air.

Convinced that there was evil magic in the air, Blacktooth's and Razor Toe's men ran for their lives before they met a similar fate. They hurled themselves from the decks and fled to the longboat, just as Razor Toe crumbled to dust.

The King is Found

It was the following day, and Princess Haree, wearing her crown, made her way victoriously through Roseberry towards her castle. Al, Jack, Mahoot and Snakeboot walked on either side of her as a crowd gathered, cheering and laughing. Al held Razor Toe's turban high so that everyone would know the cruel pirate king was dead.

That evening Haree sat on her throne as her father was brought to her, having been freed from a prison room deep within the castle. Razor Toe had tried for nearly a year to get information from the poor man about the hidden rooms and tunnels, but he had never revealed his secrets. Now his bravery was rewarded. Haree rushed into his arms and they held each other with tears in their eyes.

"I think we should give Haree and her father some space," said Jack.

"You're right," said Al. "Come on, Snakeboot, show us around the castle."

The cat led them down a splendid hallway and into a small room. As Al entered he felt the tingling in his arms and legs that he had come to know so well. He turned to see Jack shimmering, ghost-like.

Moments later the boys found themselves back in the twenty-first century, in Al's attic at number five Drake Drive. Snakeboot was with them and Al was still holding Razor Toe's turban with the glittering black diamond.

Jack reached down and patted the cat's head. "Snakeboot's come home again."

He was interrupted as the attic door swung open and Al's sister, Hally, burst into the room. Her eyes widened at the sight of Snakeboot. "You've been to the Dragon Blood Islands!" she said accusingly.

Al nodded sheepishly.

"It was really scary," said Jack. "You would have hated it."

"Hmph! Well, I'm glad I didn't go then," said Hally, crossing her arms nonetheless. "But it's great you've brought Snakeboot back with you!" she continued, softening. "I've missed him."

Snakeboot leapt towards her in greeting. She picked him up and tickled his chin, and the cat purred loudly.

When she left the room, Al looked at the black diamond on the turban. "What should I do with it?" he asked.

"Put it on the scabbard where it belongs," Jack replied.

Carefully, and not without dread, Al removed the glittering black gem and placed it between one of the sets of empty clasps on the scabbard. He bent the clasps into place so the diamond was held fast. Then he picked up the Dragon Blood Sabre and the Scabbard of Invincibility and locked them in the sea trunk.

"I'm not sure I'm happy about owning a black dragon diamond," he told Jack.

"I think Prince Alleric probably felt the same way," said Jack. "Mahoot's grandfather was right. I think the diamonds could be a curse."

"We have to be careful to use the sword and scabbard wisely," said Al. "I'd like

Mahoot's grandfather to be proud of us."

"He'll definitely be proud of us if we find the rest of Prince Alleric's missing treasure," said Jack.

"He sure will," said Al with a smile. "And Snakeboot won't rest until we return all the jewels that Vicious Victor stole from Sabre Island."

"I don't think we'll rest either," agreed Jack. "I love our adventures. I can't wait to return for more."

Captain's Code

Can you decipher the following message written in Morse code? Check out www.dragonbloodpirates.co.uk for the clues to the Captain's Code...if you dare!

$$- -.\quad ..-\quad -.\quad -.\quad .\quad .-.$$

$$-.-.\quad .-\quad -.\quad -$$

$$-...\quad .$$

$$-\quad .-.\quad ..-\quad ...\quad -\quad .\quad -..$$

Arrr! Ahoy there, mateys!
Hoist the sails and drop the anchor: ye have some treasure to find!

One swashbucklin' reader will win an ipod Touch and
ten runners up will win a Dragon Blood Pirates booty bag.
For a chance to win, ye must dare to unearth the treasure!

Each of the six Dragon Blood Pirates: **The Legend of
Dragon Island** books contain a clue.
When you have solved the six clues, enter the answers online
at www.dragonbloodpirates.co.uk

Or send your name, address and answers to:

Dragon Blood Pirates:
The Legend of Dragon Island
338 Euston Road, London NW1 3BH

Best o' luck, me hearties!

To find where the pirate treasure lies,
ye must find the answer to the clue that lies below:

**This helpful captain is wounded by Razor Toe,
As he sails our heroes wherever they wish to go.**

Only one entry per child. Final draw 31 August 2011.
For full terms and conditions visit
www.dragonbloodpirates.co.uk/terms

Don't ye miss book eight in the

Dragon Blood Pirates

series!

Turn the page and shiver yer timbers
with a slice of the next high-seas adventure...

The Scabbard of Invincibility

"Ow! That hurt," Al Breas complained, rubbing his arm.

"Sorry," said his best friend, Jack Seabrook, "but you did say to hit you hard."

"I thought I wouldn't feel any pain," said Al. "I thought the Scabbard of Invincibility with its new dragon diamond would protect me."

Their three-legged white cat, Snakeboot,

sat on an old sea trunk beside Al. He reached out with his paw and his claws caught on the glittering black diamond set in the silver scabbard hanging from Al's waist. Al unhooked the cat's claw and studied the sheath and jewel with a worried frown.

"Mahoot's grandfather said you'd have to find all four black dragon diamonds and put them back on the scabbard before it can make you invincible," Jack reminded Al.

"So, at the moment, if I'm wearing the scabbard and get knifed in the guts, I'll still be wounded," said Al, shivering at the thought.

"Yes, but you won't die unless you take the scabbard off," said Jack. "The diamond on the scabbard makes you deathless."

Al shuddered at the memory of the diamond's last owner, Razor Toe the pirate king. He had crumbled to dust when the black diamond he wore in his turban was

snatched from his head. Now the same
diamond that Razor Toe had worn glittered
from Al's scabbard.

"I don't want to end up like Razor Toe,"
said Al.

Snakeboot meowed, left the sea trunk and wound himself around Al's legs in agreement.

"Razor Toe was bad enough," said Jack, "but when we return to the Dragon Blood Islands with the sabre and scabbard, Blacktooth will want to steal them from us, too."

"What should we do?" said Al. "I do want to go back to the islands, but I'm worried..."

"Let's leave the sabre and scabbard here then," Jack suggested. He bent down and tickled Snakeboot's ear. "What do you think, Snakeboot? Should we leave them behind?"

The cat arched his back and purred loudly in answer, then leapt to the top of an old cupboard.

"I think he wants us to put them up there," said Jack. "They'd be out of reach of your little sister. Hally will never see them up there."

Al unbuckled his weapon and sheath,

climbed on a chair and placed them on top of the cupboard, away from prying eyes.

"I suppose that'll be fine," said Al, "since Vicious Victor gave us rings, too." He held out his hand to regard the ruby-eyed dragonhead ring, a gift from the pirate ghost, that glittered on his thumb. "We have to find out what they're all about."

"Who would have guessed my ring once belonged to Princess Haree of Ruby Island?" said Jack. "Or that it was a key to secret passageways? Maybe your dragon ring, Hally's pearl ring and Mahoot's elephant-head ring have secrets too."

"We know Vicious Victor wants Snakeboot to help us find Prince Alleric's lost treasures so he can finally rest in peace," Al replied, "so the rings may be keys to more treasures."

Snakeboot purred loudly and his purple eyes flashed, as if agreeing with Al. He went to the sea trunk and pawed at the lock.

"OK, that's settled then," said Jack. "I think Snakeboot's saying it's time for us to return to the Dragon Blood Islands."

Snakeboot purred again, so Al opened the sea trunk and stepped inside. Jack and the cat followed. In seconds they had vanished from Al's attic at number five Drake Drive.

Finding themselves back on Ruby Island, Al and Jack discovered that Captain Gunner and the crew of *The Dandylion* had been so busy celebrating their victory over Razor Toe that they hadn't missed the boys at all. Breathing sighs of relief, they settled back into the festivities.

A few days later, celebrations complete, a cheering crowd lined the docks as *The Dandylion* cast off and set course for the main town in the Dragon Blood Islands. Al and Jack stood on the poop deck with Gunner and their friend, Mahoot, the cabin boy, waving goodbye.

"I'm glad the king of Ruby Island is back on the throne," said Al.

"And that we sent Blacktooth running," chortled Captain Gunner. "Now I'm gunner buy some big cannons so I can blast him to kingdom come next time we see him."

"Where do you reckon Blacktooth's gone?" asked Mahoot. "He took off like a frightened rabbit when Razor Toe crumbled to dust."

"That lisping lickspittle might attack us again, especially now he knows Al's got the Dragon Blood Sabre," said Gunner. He glanced at Al's waist, looking for the sabre, and his eyebrows shot up in surprise. "Where is it?" he cried in alarm. "You haven't gone and lost it, have you?"

"Don't worry," replied Al. "I've hidden it where no one can find it."

The Treasure

While Captain Gunner was fitting new
cannons to *The Dandylion* below decks,
Stanley Spong shuffled up the gangplank.
Al and Jack, curious as to why the shifty
trader would come aboard, took him
straight down to Gunner.

"What are you doing here?" asked
Gunner, eyeing Spong suspiciously.

Spong shuffled his feet, coughed and spat.
He looked sideways at Gunner, not meeting
his eyes. "I've got some information for you,"

he said. "And it might be worth a bit."

"Tempt me," said Gunner, intrigued.

Spong's voice dropped. "Blacktooth and Snotty are both in port, and Blacktooth's hurrying to finish a special bit of work he's having done on *The Revenge* so he can leave as quickly as possible tomorrow. He knows about something that Snotty does too, and he's planning to get there first."

"What something?" asked Gunner.

"Treasure," Spong replied. "And as I'm the only one who can tell you what they know, I want a bit of the booty you've already found for myself."

Gunner reached into his pocket and pulled out a small ruby. "This is the best you'll get from me," he said, holding out the gem.

"One small ruby for a golden casket full of sapphires?" whispered Spong, and waited for Gunner to digest the bait.

"One more then – but that's it," Gunner

offered. "And the information had better be good, especially as Snotty and Blacktooth already know about it."

"So you'd be happy to let them get it all for themselves and not even try to get it yourself, would you?" asked Spong, knowing full well Gunner held a big grudge against both the other pirates – a grudge big enough to make him race them to any treasure.

Gunner grabbed another ruby. "Here, take this, and tell me what they know," he growled. The ruby sparkled in his hand and Spong's eyes flashed greedily as he took the payment, before reaching into his coat and handing Gunner two pages torn from a book. "I found this old diary that belonged to a butler who once worked in Prince Alleric's castle on Sabre Island. The man is dead, of course, and his granddaughter has been selling all his things. These pages are all you need."

With those words Spong turned on his heels and rapidly left the boat.

Gunner pored over the pages, reading aloud: "Today Prince Alleric arrived home. Terrible news! His boat is badly damaged, half his crew are butchered, and his cargo and treasure are abandoned because of a terrible fight with Vicious Victor, the evil pirate who is ravaging the Dragon Blood Islands.

"Prince Alleric fought off the pirates, but as his boat was sinking under the weight of cargo he was forced to offload his freight, including a golden casket full of sapphires, on a deserted island. Then, almost single-handedly, the prince managed to sail his ruined boat home. Later, I overheard him tell his sister, Princess Halimeda, "I've made a map of the whereabouts of the golden casket. So that the map doesn't fall into the wrong hands, I've put it in the secret drawer inside

your elephant. Here is the key. Keep it safe."
He handed his sister a strange ring, shaped
like an elephant's head, and she put it on
her finger.